Tent Tw

CW00418063

Written by Kathryn Stewart

Illustrated by Esther Hernando

"Can we spend a night in the garden?" said Bethan.

"No. It is too wet, but we can pretend!" said Bella.

"Look!" said Bella. "The bunk bed can be a tent. We can sleep in it tonight with the star light on!"

Bethan and Bella had a plan.

"We need to lift the rug up to there," said Bella.

Gran got them a sheet.

"How do we fix the sheet to the
bed, Bethan?" said Bella.

"We need some pegs," said Bethan.

"I can fix it," said Bethan. "Grip it
well. Do not let it drop."

Bethan lifted the sheet up high.

Dad and Gran inspected the tent.

"Can we have the star light on the shelf, Dad?" said Bethan and Bella.

"Can we get some milk and a little snack?" said Bethan and Bella.

"This camp is the best!" said Gran.
"Can we come in?"